678995
BOOK SET

GINGER
FEAR, SHARON

Roosevelt Elementary

GINGER

by Sharon Fear ❖ illustrated by Nancy Carpenter

GReaT SouRCe
EDUCATION GROUP
A Houghton Mifflin Company

Oh, no! Ginger needed to find a new home.

She walked all around town.
She looked up one street and
she looked down another.

Ginger saw tall buildings and short buildings.
She saw old buildings and new buildings.

Then she saw one building she liked.
She liked the grass in front and
she liked the flowers in the windows.

Ginger walked inside
and went to the first door.
A man let her in.

She looked all around.
It was very dark. Ginger was tired,
but there was no sunny place to nap.
This was not the place for Ginger.

Ginger went to the next door.
A woman let her in.

Ginger looked all around and sniffed the air.
She smelled broccoli. Ginger was hungry,
but she didn't like broccoli!
This was not the place for Ginger.

Ginger went to the next door.
A boy let her in.

Bow-wow-wow! A dog chased her out.
Ginger didn't like dogs.
Dogs didn't like Ginger, either.
This was not the place for Ginger.

Ginger went to the last door.
This time a girl let her in.
Ginger looked all around.
Good! No dog.

Ginger sniffed the air.
Good! No broccoli.

Ginger looked at the window.
She saw a nice, sunny spot.

Good! She could nap in the sun
and keep warm.

Oh, yes!
This was the place for Ginger.
It was purr . . . purr . . . perfect.